101 Nursery Rhymes and Sing-Along Songs for Kids

By Jennifer M Edwards

Table of Contents

A Candle, A Candle

A candle, a candle,
To light me to bed;
A pillow, a pillow,
To tuck up my head.

The moon is as sleepy as sleepy can be,
The stars are all pointing their fingers at me,
And Missus Hop-Robin, way up in her nest,
Is rocking her tired little babies to rest.

So give me a blanket
To tuck up my toes,
And a little soft pillow
To snuggle my nose.

A-Tisket, A-Tasket

A-tisket, a-tasket,
A green and yellow basket.
I wrote a letter to my love,
And on the way I dropped it.

I dropped it, I dropped it,
And, on the way I dropped it.
A little boy picked it up,
And put it in his pocket.

Alternative

A-tisket, a-tasket,
I've lost my yellow basket.
A little girlie picked it up,
And put it in her pocket.

She took it, she took it,
My little yellow basket.
And if she doesn't bring it back,
I think that I shall cry.

Alternative (Long Version)

A-tisket, a-tasket,
A green and yellow basket.
I wrote a letter to my love,
And on the way I dropped it.

I dropped it, I dropped it,
Yes, on the way I dropped it.
A little girlie picked it up,
And took it to the market.

She was truckin' on down the avenue,
Without a single thing to do.
She was peck, peck, peckin' all around,
When she spied it on the ground.

A-tisket, a-tasket,
She took my yellow basket.
And if she doesn't bring it back,
I think that I shall cry.

A-tisket, a-tasket,
A green and yellow basket.
I wrote a letter to my love,
And on the way I dropped it.

I dropped it, I dropped it,
Yes, on the way I dropped it.
A little girlie picked it up,
And took it to the market.

(Was it red?) No, no, no, no
(Was it brown?) No, no, no, no
(Was it blue?) No, no, no, no
Just a little yellow basket,
A Little Yellow Basket!

A Wise Old Owl

A wise old owl sat in an oak
The more he heard, the less he spoke
The less he spoke, the more he heard
Why aren't we all like that wise old bird?

After A Bath

After a bath, I try, try, try,
To wipe myself till I'm dry, dry, dry.
Hands to wipe, and fingers and toes,
And two wet legs and a shiny nose.
Just think how much less time I'd take,
If I were a dog, and could shake, shake, shake!

Alphabet Song

A - B - C - D - E - F - G
H - I - J - K - L - M - N - O - P
Q - R - S - T - U - V
W - X - Y and Z

Now I know my ABC's
Next time won't you sing with me?

Baa, Baa, Black Sheep

Baa, baa, black sheep, have you any wool?
Yes sir, yes sir, three bags full.
One for the master, one for the dame,
And one for the little boy who lives down the lane.

Baa, baa, black sheep, have you any wool?
Yes sir, yes sir, three bags full.
One for the master, one for the dame,
And one for the little boy who lives down the lane.

Big Bad Wolf

Who's afraid of the big bad wolf?
The big bad wolf
The big bad wolf
Who's afraid of the big bad wolf?
Tra-la-la-la-la-la

I'm not afraid of the big bad wolf
The big bad wolf
The big bad wolf
I'm not afraid of the big bad wolf
Tra-la-la-la-la-la

B-I-N-G-O

There was a farmer had a dog,
And Bingo was his name-o.
B-I-N-G-O!
B-I-N-G-O!
B-I-N-G-O!
And Bingo was his name-o!

There was a farmer had a dog,
And Bingo was his name-o.
(Clap)-I-N-G-O!
(Clap)-I-N-G-O!
(Clap)-I-N-G-O!
And Bingo was his name-o!

There was a farmer had a dog,
And Bingo was his name-o.
(Clap, clap)-N-G-O!
(Clap, clap)-N-G-O!
(Clap, clap)-N-G-O!
And Bingo was his name-o!

There was a farmer had a dog,
And Bingo was his name-o.

(Clap, clap, clap)-G-O!
(Clap, clap, clap)-G-O!
(Clap, clap, clap)-G-O!
And Bingo was his name-o!

There was a farmer had a dog,
And Bingo was his name-o.
(Clap, clap, clap, clap)-O!
(Clap, clap, clap, clap)-O!
(Clap, clap, clap, clap)-O!
And Bingo was his name-o!

There was a farmer had a dog,
And Bingo was his name-o.
(Clap, clap, clap, clap, clap)!
(Clap, clap, clap, clap, clap)!
(Clap, clap, clap, clap, clap)!
And Bingo was his name-o!

Boys and Girls Come Out to Play

Boys and girls come out to play,
the moon doth shine as bright as day.

Leave your supper and leave your sleep,
and join your play fellows in the street.

Come with a whoop and come with a call,
come with good will or not at all.

Up the ladder and down the wall,
a half-penny loaf will serve us all.

You find milk and I'll find flour,
and we'll have pudding in half an hour.

Come Let's to Bed

Come let's to bed, says Sleepy-head,
Tarry a while, says Sow,
Put on the pan, says Greedy Nan,
Let's sup before we go.

Come to the Window

Come to the window,
My baby, with me,
And look at the stars
That shine on the sea!

There are two little stars
That play bo-peep,
With two little fish
Far down in the deep;

And two little frogs
Cry "Neap, neap, neap;"
I see a dear baby
That should be asleep.

Cry Baby Bunting

Cry Baby Bunting
Daddy's gone a-hunting
Gone to fetch a rabbit skin
To wrap the Baby Bunting in
Cry Baby Bunting

Alternative

Bye, baby bumpkin,
Where's Tony Lumpkin?
My lady's on her death-bed,
For eating half a pumpkin.

Dickery, Dickery, Dare

Dickery, dickery, dare,
The pig flew up in the air.
The man in brown
Soon brought him down!
Dickery, dickery, dare.

Note:

This rhyme is often used as the second verse of
Hickory Dickory Dock (page 14).

Diddle, Diddle, Dumpling

Diddle, diddle, dumping,
My son, John,
Went to bed
With his trousers on,

One shoe off
and one shoe on!
Diddle, diddle, dumpling,
my son, John!

Variation

Stockings can be used instead of the word trousers.

Do You Know the Muffin Man?

Do you know the Muffin Man?
The Muffin Man,
The Muffin Man?

Do you know the Muffin Man?
Who lives in Drury Lane?

Yes, I know the Muffin Man,
The Muffin Man,
The Muffin Man.

Yes, I know the Muffin Man
Who lives in Drury Lane.

Eeny Meeny Miny Moe

Eeny, meeny, miny, moe
Catch a tiger by the toe
If he hollers let him go,
Eeny, meeny, miny, moe.

My mother told me
To pick the very best one
And you are [not] it.

Alternative

Eeny, meeny, miny, moe
Catch a tiger by the toe
If he hollers let him go,
Eeny, meeny, miny, moe.

Out goes one
Out goes two
Out goes another one
And that is you.

Fee! Fie! Foe! Fum!

Fee! Fie! Foe! Fum!
I smell the blood of an Englishman.
Be he 'live, or be he dead,
I'll grind his bones to make my bread.

Fiddle Dee Dee

Fiddle dee dee, fiddle dee dee,
The fly has married the bumblebee.
They went to the church,
And married was she.
The fly has married the bumblebee.

Five Little Ducks

Five little ducks went swimming one day,
Over the hills and far away.
The mother duck said 'Quack, quack, quack!'
And only four little ducks came back.

Four little ducks went swimming one day,
Over the hills and far away.
The mother duck said 'Quack, quack, quack!'
And only three little ducks came back.

Three little ducks went swimming one day,
Over the hills and far away.
The mother duck said 'Quack, quack, quack!'
And only two little ducks came back.

Two little ducks went swimming one day,
Over the hills and far away.
The mother duck said 'Quack, quack, quack!'
And only one little duck came back.

One little duck went swimming one day,
Over the hills and far away.
The mother duck said 'Quack, quack, quack!'
And all her five little ducks came back.

Five Little Speckled Frogs

Five little speckled frogs,
Sat on a speckled log,
Eating some most delicious bugs.
Yum, yum!
One jumped into the pool,
Where he was nice and cool,
Then there were four speckled frogs.
Glug, glug!

Four little speckled frogs,
Sat on a speckled log,
Eating some most delicious bugs.
Yum, yum!
One jumped into the pool,
Where he was nice and cool,
Then there were three speckled frogs.
Glug, glug!

Three little speckled frogs,
Sat on a speckled log,
Eating some most delicious bugs.
Yum, yum!
One jumped into the pool,

Where he was nice and cool,
Then there were two speckled frogs.
Glug, glug!

Two little speckled frogs,
Sat on a speckled log,
Eating some most delicious bugs.
Yum, yum!
One jumped into the pool,
Where he was nice and cool,
Then there was one speckled frog.
Glug, glug!

One little speckled frog,
Sat on a speckled log,
Eating some most delicious bugs.
Yum, yum!
He jumped into the pool,
Where he was nice and cool,
Then there were no speckled frogs.

Georgie Porgie

Georgie Porgie, puddin' and pie,
Kissed the girls and made them cry.
When the boys came out to play,
Georgie Porgie ran away.

Go to Bed First

Go to bed first, a golden purse;
Go to bed second, a golden pheasant;
Go to bed third, a golden bird.

Good Night, Sleep Tight

Good night, sleep tight,
Wake up bright
In the morning light
To do what's right
With all your might.

Alternative

Good night, sleep tight,
Don't let the bedbugs bite
But if they do
Beat them with your shoe
'Til they're black and blue

Head, Shoulders, Knees and Toes

Head, shoulders, knees and toes,
Knees and toes
Head, shoulders, knees and toes,
Knees and toes

And eyes and ears and mouth and nose
Head, shoulders, knees and toes

Alternative (Long Version)

Head and shoulders, knees and toes,
Knees and toes,
Knees and toes,
Head and shoulders, knees and toes,
It's my body.

Eyes and ears and mouth and nose,
Mouth and nose,
Mouth and nose,
Eyes and ears and mouth and nose,
It's my body.

Ankles, elbows, feet and seat,
Feet and seat,
Feet and seat,
Ankles, elbows, feet and seat,
It's my body.

Hey Diddle Diddle

Hey diddle diddle, the cat and the fiddle,
The cow jumped over the moon.
The little dog laughed to see such fun
And the dish ran away with the spoon!

Hickory, Dickory, Dock

Hickory, dickory, dock,
The mouse ran up the clock.
The clock struck one,
The mouse ran down!
Hickory, dickory, dock.

Variation

Replace the line "The mouse ran down!" with "And
down he run"

Note:

Dickory Dickory Dare (page 14) is often used as the
second verse.

Higglety Pigglety

Higglety, pigglety, my black hen,
She lays eggs for gentlemen.

Sometimes nine, and sometimes ten,
Higglety, pigglety, my black hen.

Alternative

Higgledy Piggledy, my black hen,
She lays eggs for gentlemen;

Gentlemen come every day,
To see what my black hen doth lay.

Sometimes nine, and sometimes ten,
Higgledy Piggledy, my black hen!

Higglety, Pigglety, Pop

Higglety, Pigglety, Pop,
The dog has eaten the mop.
The pig's in a hurry,
The cat's in a flurry,
Higglety, Pigglety, Pop.

Hokey-Pokey

You put your right foot in,
You put your right foot out;
You put your right foot in,
And you shake it all about.
You do the Hokey-Pokey,
And you turn yourself around.
That's what it's all about!

You put our left foot in,
You put your left foot out;
You put your left foot in,
And you shake it all about.
You do the Hokey-Pokey,
And you turn yourself around.
That's what it's all about!

You put your right hand in,
You put your right hand out;
You put your right hand in,
And you shake it all about.
You do the Hokey-Pokey,
And you turn yourself around.
That's what it's all about!

You put your left hand in,
You put your left hand out;
You put your left hand in,
And you shake it all about.
You do the Hokey-Pokey,
And you turn yourself around.
That's what it's all about!

You put your right side in,
You put your right side out;
You put your right side in,
And you shake it all about.
You do the Hokey-Pokey,
And you turn yourself around.
That's what it's all about!

You put your left side in,
You put your left side out;
You put your left side in,
And you shake it all about.
You do the Hokey-Pokey,
And you turn yourself around.
That's what it's all about!

You put your nose in,
You put your nose out;
You put your nose in,
And you shake it all about.
You do the Hokey-Pokey,
And you turn yourself around.
That's what it's all about!

You put your tail (or backside) in,
You put your tail out;
You put your tail in,
And you shake it all about.
You do the Hokey-Pokey,
And you turn yourself around.
That's what it's all about!

You put your head in,
You put your head out;
You put your head in,
And you shake it all about.
You do the Hokey-Pokey,
And you turn yourself around.
That's what it's all about!

You put your whole self in,
You put your whole self out;
You put your whole self in,
And you shake it all about.
You do the Hokey-Pokey,
And you turn yourself around.
That's what it's all about!

Humpty Dumpty

Humpty Dumpty sat on a wall.
Humpty Dumpty had a great fall.
All the king's horses and all the king's men,
Couldn't put Humpty together again!

Hush Little Baby

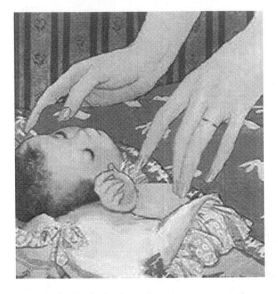

Hush, little baby, don't say a word,
Mama's gonna buy you a mockin'bird.

If that mockin'bird don't sing,
Mama's gonna buy you a diamond ring.

If that diamond ring turns brass,
Mama's gonna buy you a looking glass.

If that looking glass gets broke,
Mama's gonna buy you a billy goat.

If that billy goat don't pull,
Mama's gonna buy you a cart and bull.

If that cart and bull turn over,
Mama's gonna buy you a dog named Rover.

If that dog named Rover won't bark,
Mama's gonna buy you a horse and cart.

If that horse and cart fall down,
Then you'll be the sweetest little baby in town.

Variation

Changing the line "If that cart and bull turn over" to "If that cart and bull fall down", then saying the last line of the rhyme. This would omit all the lines in between.

I Scream

I scream,
You scream,
We all scream,
For ice cream!

I See the Moon

I see the moon,
And the moon sees me.
The moon sees the somebody I'd like to see.

God bless the moon,
And God bless me.
God bless the somebody I'd like to see!

I'm A Little Teapot

I'm a little teapot, short and stout,
Here is my handle (one hand on hip),
here is my spout (other arm out straight).

When I get all steamed up, hear me shout,
Just tip me over and pour me out!
(As song ends, lean over and tip arm out like a spout)

I'm a clever teapot, yes it's true,
Here's an example of what I can do;
I can change my handle to my spout,
(switch arm positions and repeat tipping motion)
Just tip me over and pour me out.

I've Been Workin' on the Railroad

I've been workin' on the railroad,
All the live long day.
I've been workin' on the railroad,
Just to pass the time away.
Don't you hear the whistle blowing?
Rise up so early in the morn.
Don't you hear the captain shouting
"Dinah, blow your horn?"

Dinah, won't you blow,
Dinah, won't you blow,
Dinah, won't you blow your horn?
Dinah, won't you blow,
Dinah, won't you blow,
Dinah, won't you blow your horn?

Someone's in the kitchen with Dinah.
Someone's in the kitchen, I know.
Someone's in the kitchen with Dinah
Strumming on the old banjo.Fee, fie, fiddle-e-i-o.
Fee, fie, fiddle-e-i-o-o-o-o.
Fee, fie, fiddle-e-i-o.
Strumming on the old banjo.

If You're Happy and You Know It

If you're happy and you know it,
Clap your hands (clap clap)
If you're happy and you know it,
Clap your hands (clap clap)
If you're happy and you know it,
Then your face will surely show it
If you're happy and you know it,
Clap your hands. (clap clap)

If you're happy and you know it,
Stomp your feet (stomp stomp)
If you're happy and you know it,
Stomp your feet (stomp stomp)
If you're happy and you know it,
Then your face will surely show it
If you're happy and you know it,
Stomp your feet. (stomp stomp)

If you're happy and you know it,
Shout "Hurray!" (hoo-ray!)
If you're happy and you know it,
Shout "Hurray!" (hoo-ray!)
If you're happy and you know it,
Then your face will surely show it
If you're happy and you know it,
Shout "Hurray!" (hoo-ray!)

If you're happy and you know it,
Do all three (clap-clap, stomp-stomp, hoo-ray!)
If you're happy and you know it,
Do all three (clap-clap, stomp-stomp, hoo-ray!)
If you're happy and you know it,
Then your face will surely show it
If you're happy and you know it,
Do all three. (clap-clap, stomp-stomp, hoo-ray!)

It's Raining, It's Pouring

It's raining, it's pouring,
The old man is snoring.
He went to bed and he bumped his head,
And he couldn't get up in the morning.

Alternative 1

It's raining, it's pouring,
The old man is snoring.
He went to bed to rest his head,
And he never got up again.

Alternative 2

It's raining, it's pouring,
The old man is snoring.
Bumped his head
As he went to bed
And he couldn't get up in the morning.

Itsy Bitsy Spider

The itsy bitsy spider
Went up the water spout,
Down came the rain
And washed the spider out.

Out came the sun
And dried up all the rain,
And the itsy bitsy spider
Went up the spout again.

Variation

You could say "crawled" instead of "went" up the
water spout.

Also, some versions use "incy wincy" or "ency
weensy" instead of itsy bitsy.

Jack and Jill

Jack and Jill,
Went up the hill,
To fetch a pail of water.
Jack fell down,
And broke his crown,
And Jill came tumbling after.

Up Jack got,
And home did trot,
As fast as he could caper.
Went to bed,
And plastered his head,
With vinegar and brown paper.

Jack Be Nimble

Jack, be nimble,
Jack, be quick,
Jack, jump over
The candlestick.

Jack jumped high,
Jack jumped low,
Jack jumped over
and burned his toe.

Little Betty Blue

Little Betty Blue,
Lost her holiday shoe;
What shall little Betty do?
Giver her anther,
To match the other,
And then she'll walk upon two.

Variation

The last line can also be,
"And then she may walk in two."

Little Bo Peep

Little Bo Peep has lost her sheep,
And doesn't know where to find them.
Leave them alone and they'll come home,
Wagging their tails behind them.

Note

The second line could also read, "And can't tell where
to find them."

Alternative (Long Version)

Little Bo Peep has lost her sheep,
And can't tell where to find them.
Leave them alone and they'll come home,
Wagging their tails behind them.

Little Bo Peep fell fast asleep,
And dreamt she heard them bleating;
But when she awoke, she found it a joke,
For they were all still fleeting.

Then up she took her little crook,
Determined for to find them;
She found them indeed, but it made her heart bleed,
For they'd left all their tails behind them.

It happened one day, as Boo Peep did stray,
Into a meadow hard by,
There she espied their tails side by side,
All hung on a tree to dry.

She heaved a sigh, and wiped her eye,
And over the hillocks went rambling,
And tried what she could, as a shepherdess should,
To tack again each to its lambkin.

Little Boy Blue

Little Boy Blue, come blow your horn,
The sheep's in the meadow, the cow's in the corn.
Where is the boy who looks after the sheep?
He's under a haycock, fast asleep.
Will you wake him? No, not I,
For if I do, he's sure to cry.

Little Bunny Foo Foo

Little Bunny Foo Foo,
Hopping through the forest
Scooping up the field mice
And bopping them on the head.

Down came the Good Fairy, and she said,

"Little bunny Foo Foo,
I don't want to see you
Scooping up the field mice
And bopping them on the head."

Alternative (Long Version)

Little Bunny Foo Foo,
Hopping through the forest
Scooping up the field mice
And bopping them on the head.

Down came the Good Fairy, and she said,

"Little bunny Foo Foo,
I don't want to see you
Scooping up the field mice
And bopping them on the head.
I'll give you three chances,

And if you don't behave
I'll turn you into a goon!"

The next day:

Little Bunny Foo Foo,
Hopping through the forest
Scooping up the field mice
And bopping them on the head.

Down came the Good Fairy, and she said,

"Little bunny Foo Foo,
I don't want to see you
Scooping up the field mice
And bopping them on the head.
I'll give you two more chances,
And if you don't behave
I'll turn you into a goon!"

The next day:

Little Bunny Foo Foo,
Kept hopping through the forest
Kept scooping up the field mice
And bopping them on the head.

Down came the Good Fairy, and she said,

"Little bunny Foo Foo,
I don't want to see you
Scooping up the field mice
And bopping them on the head.
I'll give you one more chance,
And if you don't behave
I'll turn you into a goon!"

The next day:

Little Bunny Foo Foo,
Kept hopping through the forest

Kept scooping up the field mice
And bopping them on the head.

Down came the Good Fairy, and she said,

"Little bunny Foo Foo,
I don't want to see you
Scooping up the field mice
And bopping them on the head.
I gave you three chances,
And if you didn't behave
Now you're a goon! POOF!"

The moral of the story is:
HARE TODAY, GOON TOMORROW

Little Jack Horner

Little Jack Horner
Sat in a corner,
Eating a mincemeat pie.
He stuck in his thumb
And pulled out a plum,
And said, "What a good boy am I!"

Variation

You can have Jack eating a Christmas pie instead of a
mincemeat pie.

Little King Boggen

Little King Boggen, he built a fine new hall;
Pastry and piecrust, that was the wall;
The windows were made of black pudding and white,
Roofed with pancakes, you never saw the like.

Variation

Instead of "Roofed", you could use "And shingled"
or "And slated" instead.

Little Miss Muffet

Little Miss Muffet,
Sat on a tuffet,
Eating her curds and whey;

Along came a spider,
Who sat down beside her,
And frightened Miss Muffet away.

London Bridge is Falling Down

London Bridge is falling down,
Falling down, falling down.
London Bridge is falling down,
My fair lady.

Take a key and lock her up,
Lock her up, lock her up.
Take a key and lock her up,
My fair lady.

How will we build it up,
Build it up, build it up?
How will we build it up,
My fair lady?

Build it up with silver and gold,
Silver and gold, silver and gold.
Build it up with silver and gold,
My fair lady.

Gold and silver I have none,
I have none, I have none.

Gold and silver I have none,
My fair lady.

Build it up with needles and pins,
Needles and pins, needles and pins.
Build it up with needles and pins,
My fair lady.

Pins and needles bend and break,
Bend and break, bend and break.
Pins and needles bend and break,
My fair lady.

Build it up with wood and clay,
Wood and clay, wood and clay.
Build it up with wood and clay,
My fair lady.

Wood and clay will wash away,
Wash away, wash away.
Wood and clay will wash away,
My fair lady.

Build it up with stone so strong,
Stone so strong, stone so strong.
Build it up with stone so strong,
My fair lady.

Stone so strong will last so long,
Last so long, last so long.
Stone so strong will last so long,
My fair lady.

Lucy Locket

Lucy Locket lost her pocket,
Kitty Fisher found it;
Not a penny was there in it,
Only ribbon round it.

Lullaby and Goodnight

Lullaby and goodnight, with roses bedight
With lilies o'er spread is baby's wee bed
Lay thee down now and rest, may thy slumber be blessed
Lay thee down now and rest, may thy slumber be blessed

Lullaby and goodnight, thy mother's delight
Bright angels beside my darling abide
They will guard thee at rest, thou shalt wake on my breast
They will guard thee at rest, thou shalt wake on my breast

Mary Had A Little Lamb

Mary had a little lamb,
Little lamb, little lamb,
Mary had a little lamb,
Its fleece was white as snow.

And everywhere that Mary went,
Mary went, Mary went,
And everywhere that Mary went,
The lamb was sure to go.

It followed her to school one day,
school one day, school one day,
It followed her to school one day,
Which was against the rules.

It made the children laugh and play,
Laugh and play, laugh and play,

It made the children laugh and play,
To see a lamb at school.

And so the teacher turned it out,
Turned it out, turned it out,
And so the teacher turned it out,
But still it lingered near.

And waited patiently about,
Patiently about, patiently about,
And waited patiently about,
Till Mary did appear.

"Why does the lamb love Mary so?"
Love Mary so? Love Mary so?
"Why does the lamb love Mary so,"
The eager children cry.

"Why, Mary loves the lamb, you know."
The lamb, you know, the lamb, you know,
"Why, Mary loves the lamb, you know,"
The teacher did reply.

Monday's Child

Monday's child is fair of face,
Tuesday's child is full of grace,
Wednesday's child is full of woe,
Thursday's child has far to go,
Friday's child is loving and giving,
Saturday's child must work for a living,
But the child that's born on the Sabbath day,
Is fair and wise and good and gay.

Oh Where, Oh Where Has My Little Dog Gone

Oh where, oh where has my little dog gone?
Oh where, oh where can he be?
With his ears cut short and his tail cut long,
Oh where, oh where can he be?

Alternative (Long Version)

Oh where, oh where has my little dog gone?
Oh where, oh where can he be?
With his ears cut short and his tail cut long,
Oh where, oh where can he be?

I think he went down to the building site,
To see what he could see.
And in his mouth was a globe so bright,
I wonder what could it be.

Oh where, oh where has my little dog gone?
Oh where, oh where can he be?

With his ears cut short and his tail cut long,
Oh where, oh where can he be?

I last saw him by the bulldozer,
Playing and running around.
But I just can't see him there anymore,
He just can't seem to be found.

Perhaps the man over there will know,
He may have seen him go by.
Who knows where he might have decided to go,
But we've got to give it a try.

Oh where, oh where has my little dog gone?
Oh where, oh where can he be?
With his ears cut short and his tail cut long,
Oh where, oh where can he be?

Old MacDonald

Old MacDonald had a farm, E-I-E-I-O
And on his farm he had a cow, E-I-E-I-O
With a moo, moo here and a moo, moo there
Here a moo there a moo
Everywhere a moo, moo
Old MacDonald had a farm, E-I-E-I-O

Old MacDonald had a farm, E-I-E-I-O
And on his farm he had a pig, E-I-E-I-O
With an oink, oink here and an oink, oink there
Here an oink, there an oink
Everywhere an oink, oink
With a moo, moo here and a moo, moo there
Here a moo there a moo
Everywhere a moo, moo
Old MacDonald had a farm, E-I-E-I-O

Old MacDonald had a farm, E-I-E-I-O
And on his farm he had a horse, E-I-E-I-O
With a neigh, neigh here and a neigh, neigh there

Here a neigh, there a neigh
Everywhere a neigh, neigh
With an oink, oink here and an oink, oink there
Here an oink, there an oink
Everywhere an oink, oink
With a moo, moo here and a moo, moo there
Here a moo there a moo
Everywhere a moo, moo
Old MacDonald had a farm, E-I-E-I-O

Old Mother Hubbard

Old Mother Hubbard
Went to the cupboard
To fetch her poor dog a bone;
But when she came there
The cupboard was bare,
And so the poor dog had none.

She took a clean dish
To get him some tripe;
But when she came back
He was smoking a pipe.

She went to the grocer's
To buy him some fruit;
But when she came back
He was playing the flute.

She went to the baker's
To buy him some bread;
But when she came back
The poor dog was dead.

She went to the undertaker's
To buy him a coffin;
But when she came back
The poor dog was laughing.

She went to the hatter's
To buy him a hat;
But when she came back
He was feeding the cat.

The dame made a curtsey,
The dog made a bow;
The dame said, "Your servant."
The dog said, "Bow wow!"

One Misty, Moisty Morning

One misty, moisty morning,
When cloudy was the weather,
I chanced to meet an old man,
Clothed all in leather.

He began to compliment,
And I began to grin,
How do you do?
And how do you do?
And how do you do, again?

One, Two, Buckle My Shoe

One, two,
Buckle my shoe;

Three, four,
Shut the door;

Five, six,
Pick up sticks;

Seven, eight,
Lay them straight;

Nine, ten,
A big fat hen;

Eleven, twelve,
Dig and delve;

Thirteen, fourteen,
Maids a-courting;

Fifteen, sixteen,
Maids in the kitchen;

Seventeen, eighteen,
Maids in waiting;

Nineteen, twenty,
My plate's empty.

Variation

For three, four, you could say "knock at the door",
and for nineteen, twenty, you could say "I've had
plenty".

One, Two, Three, Four, Five

One, two, three, four, five,
Once I caught a fish alive.
Six, seven, eight, nine, ten,
Then I let it go again.
Why did you let it go?
Because it bit my finger so.
Which finger did it bite?
This little finger on the right.

One, two, three, four, five,
Once I caught a fish alive.
Six, seven, eight, nine, ten,
Then I let it go again.
Why did you let it go?
Because it bit my finger so.
Which finger did it bite?
This little finger on the right.

Pat-A-Cake

Pat-a-cake, pat-a-cake, baker's man,
Bake me a cake as fast as you can.
Roll it, and prick it, and mark it with a "B"
And put it in the oven for Baby and me!

Variation

You replace the "B" with the first letter of any name,
and replace "Baby" with the same name.

Peter, Peter, Pumpkin Eater

Peter, Peter, pumpkin eater,
Had a wife and couldn't keep her.
He put her in a pumpkin shell,
And there he kept her, very well.

Peter Piper

Peter Piper picked a peck
Of pickled peppers;
A peck of pickled peppers
Peter Piper picked.

If Peter Piper picked a peck
Of pickled peppers.
Where's the peck of pickled peppers
Peter Piper picked?

Polly, Put the Kettle On

Polly, put the kettle on,
Polly, put the kettle on,
Polly, put the kettle on,
We'll all have tea.

Sukey, take it off again,
Sukey, take it off again,
Sukey, take it off again,
They've all gone away.

Blow the fire and make the toast,
Put the muffins on to roast,
Blow the fire and make the toast,
We'll all have tea.

Pop! Goes the Weasel

Round and round the cobbler's bench
The monkey chased the weasel,
The monkey thought 'twas all in fun
Pop! Goes the weasel.

A penny for a spool of thread
A penny for a needle,
That's the way the money goes,
Pop! Goes the weasel.

A half a pound of tupenny rice,
A half a pound of treacle.
Mix it up and make it nice,
Pop! Goes the weasel.

Up and down the London road,
In and out the Eagle,
That's the way the money goes,
Pop! Goes the weasel.

I've no time to plead and pine,
I've no time to wheedle,
Kiss me quick and then I'm gone
Pop! Goes the weasel.

Alternative

Half a pound of tupenny rice,
Half a pound of treacle.
That's the way the money goes,
Pop! Goes the weasel.

Up and down the city road,
In and out the Eagle,
That's the way the money goes,
Pop! Goes the weasel.

Modern Alternative

All around the cobbler's bench
The monkey chased the weasel,
The monkey thought 'twas all in fun
Pop! Goes the weasel.

A penny for a spool of thread
A penny for a needle,
That's the way the money goes,
Pop! Goes the weasel.

Jimmy's got the whooping cough,
And Timmy's got the measles.
That's the way the story goes,
Pop! Goes the weasel.

Rain, Rain, Go Away

Rain, rain, go away,
Come again another day;
Little Johnny wants to play.

Note:

Johnny can be substituted for any boy or girl name.

Ring A-Round the Roses

Ring a-round the roses,
A pocket full of posies,
Ashes! Ashes!
We all fall down!

Note:

The above rhyme is the most modern version. The
traditional version is as follows.

Alternative

Ring-a-ring o' roses,
A pocket full of posies,
Achoo! Achoo!
We all fall down.

Rock-A-Bye Baby

Rock-a-bye baby
In the tree top,
When the wind blows
The cradle will rock,
When the bough breaks
The cradle will fall,
And down will come baby,
Cradle and all.

Baby is drowsing
Cosy and fair,
Mother sits near
In her rocking chair,
Forward and back
The cradle she swings,
And though baby sleeps
He hears what she sings.

From the high rooftops
Down to the sea,
No one's as dear
As baby to me,
Wee little fingers
Eyes wide and bright,

Now sound asleep
Until morning light.

Alternative

Hush-a-bye, baby,
In the tree top.

When the wind blows,
The cradle will rock.

When the bough breaks,
The cradle will fall,

And down will come baby,
Cradle and all.

Row, Row, Row Your Boat

Row, row, row your boat,
Gently down the stream.
Merrily, merrily, merrily, merrily,
Life is but a dream.

She'll Be Comin' Round the Mountain

She'll be comin' round the mountain
When she comes,
(When she comes).
She'll be comin' round the mountain
When she comes,
(When she comes).
She'll be comin' round the mountain,
She'll be comin' round the mountain,
She'll be comin' round the mountain,
When she comes,
(When she comes).

She'll be drivin' six white horses
When she comes,
(When she comes).
She'll be drivin' six white horses
When she comes,
(When she comes).
She'll be drivin' six white horses,
She'll be drivin' six white horses,
She'll be drivin' six white horses,
When she comes,
(When she comes).

Oh, we'll all go out to greet her
When she comes,
(When she comes).
Oh, we'll all go out to greet her

When she comes,
(When she comes).
Oh, we'll all go out to greet her,
Oh, we'll all go out to greet her,
Oh, we'll all go out to greet her,
When she comes,
(When she comes).

Six Little Mice

Six little mice sat down to spin;
Pussy passed by and she peeped in;
"What are you doing, my little men?"
"Weaving coats for gentlemen."
"Shall I come in and cut off your threads?"
"No, no, Mistress Pussy, you'd bite of our heads."
"Oh, no, I'll not; I'll help you to spin."
"That may be so, but you don't come in!"

Skip to My Lou

Skip, skip, skip to my Lou,
Skip, skip, skip to my Lou,
Skip, skip, skip to my Lou,
Skip, to my Lou, my darlin'.

Fly's in the buttermilk, shoo, shoo, shoo,
Fly's in the buttermilk, shoo, shoo, shoo,
Fly's in the buttermilk, shoo, shoo, shoo,
Skip, to my Lou, my darlin'.

Sleep, Baby, Sleep

Sleep, baby, sleep,
Thy papa guards the sheep;
Thy mama shakes the dreamland tree,
And from it fall sweet dreams for thee,
Sleep, baby, sleep.

Sleep, baby, sleep,
Our cottage vale is deep;
The little lamb is on the green,
With woolly fleece so soft and clean,
Sleep, baby, sleep.

Sleep, baby, sleep,
Down where the woodbines creep;
Be always like the lamb so mild,
A kind and sweet and gentle child,
Sleep, baby, sleep.

Smiling Girls, Rosy Boys

Smiling girls, rosy boys,
Come and buy my little toys;
Monkeys made of gingerbread,
And sugar horses painted red.

Sneezing

If you sneeze on Monday, you sneeze for danger,
Sneeze on a Tuesday, kiss a stranger,
Sneeze on a Wednesday, sneeze for a letter,
Sneeze on a Thursday, something better,
Sneeze on a Friday, sneeze for sorrow,
Sneeze on a Saturday, joy to-morrow.

Somewhere Over the Rainbow

Somewhere, over the rainbow, way up high,
There's a land that I heard of once in a lullaby.
Somewhere, over the rainbow, skies are blue,
And the dreams that you dare to dream,
Really do come true.

One day I'll wish upon a star,
And wake up where the clouds are far behind me.
Where troubles melt like lemon drops,
Away above the chimney tops,
That's where you'll find me.

Somewhere over the rainbow, bluebirds fly,
Birds fly over the rainbow,
Why, oh why can't I?

Where troubles melt like lemon drops,
Away above the chimney tops,
That's where you'll find me.

Somewhere over the rainbow, bluebirds fly,
Birds fly over the rainbow,
Why then, oh why can't I?

Star Light, Star Bright

Star light, star bright,
First star I see tonight,
I wish I may, I wish I might,
Have the wish I wish tonight.

Teddy Bear, Teddy Bear

Teddy bear, Teddy bear,
Touch the ground.
Teddy bear, Teddy bear,
Turn around.
Teddy bear, Teddy bear,
Show your shoe.
Teddy bear, Teddy bear,
That will do.
Teddy bear, Teddy bear,
Run upstairs.
Teddy bear, Teddy bear,
Say your prayers.
Teddy bear, Teddy bear,
Blow out the light.
Teddy bear, Teddy bear,
Say good night.

Alternative

Teddy bear, Teddy bear,
Touch the ground.
Teddy bear, Teddy bear,
Turn around.
Teddy bear, Teddy bear,
Touch your nose.
Teddy bear, Teddy bear,
Tickle your toes.

Teddy Bears' Picnic

If you go down in the woods today,
You're sure of a big surprise.
If you go down in the woods today,
You'd better go in disguise.

For every bear that ever there was
Will gather there for certain because
Today's the day the Teddy Bears have their picnic.

Every Teddy Bear who's been good
Is sure of a treat today.
There's lots of marvelous things to eat
And wonderful games to play.

Beneath the trees where nobody sees
They'll hide and seek as long as they please
'Cause that's the way the Teddy Bears have their
picnic.

If you go down in the woods today,
You'd better not go alone.
It's lovely down in the woods today,
But safer to stay at home.

For every bear that ever there was
Will gather there for certain because
Today's the day the Teddy Bears have their picnic.

Picnic time for Teddy Bears...
The little Teddy Bears are having a lovely time today.
Watch them, catch them unawares,
And see them picnic on their holiday.

See them gaily gad about.
They love to play and shout.
They never have any care.

At six o'clock their Mummies and Daddies
Will take them home to bed,
Because they're tired little Teddy Bears.

Ten Little Monkeys Jumping on the Bed

Ten little monkeys jumping on the bed,
One jumped up and bumped his head,
Mom called the doctor and the doctor said,
"No more monkeys jumping on the bed."

Nine little monkeys jumping on the bed,
One jumped up and bumped his head,
Mom called the doctor and the doctor said,
"No more monkeys jumping on the bed."

Eight little monkeys jumping on the bed,
One jumped up and bumped his head,
Mom called the doctor and the doctor said,
"No more monkeys jumping on the bed."

Seven little monkeys jumping on the bed,
One jumped up and bumped his head,
Mom called the doctor and the doctor said,
"No more monkeys jumping on the bed."

Six little monkeys jumping on the bed,
One jumped up and bumped his head,
Mom called the doctor and the doctor said,
"No more monkeys jumping on the bed."

Five little monkeys jumping on the bed,
One jumped up and bumped his head,
Mom called the doctor and the doctor said,
"No more monkeys jumping on the bed."

Four little monkeys jumping on the bed,
One jumped up and bumped his head,
Mom called the doctor and the doctor said,
"No more monkeys jumping on the bed."

Three little monkeys jumping on the bed,
One jumped up and bumped his head,
Mom called the doctor and the doctor said,
"No more monkeys jumping on the bed."

Two little monkeys jumping on the bed,
One jumped up and bumped his head,
Mom called the doctor and the doctor said,
"No more monkeys jumping on the bed."

One little monkey jumping on the bed,
One jumped up and bumped his head,
Mom called the doctor and the doctor said,
"No more monkeys jumping on the bed."

The Ants Go Marching

The ants go marching one by one.
Hurrah! Hurrah!
The ants go marching one by one.
Hurrah! Hurrah!
The ants go marching one by one,
The little one stops to suck his thumb,
And they all go marching
Down
Into the ground
To get out
Of the rain.
Boom, boom, boom!

The ants go marching two by two.
Hurrah! Hurrah!
The ants go marching two by two.
Hurrah! Hurrah!
The ants go marching two by two,
The little one stops to tie his shoe,
And they all go marching
Down
Into the ground
To get out
Of the rain.
Boom, boom, boom!

The ants go marching three by three.
Hurrah! Hurrah!

The ants go marching three by three.
Hurrah! Hurrah!
The ants go marching three by three,
The little one stops to ride a bee,
And they all go marching
Down
Into the ground
To get out
Of the rain.
Boom, boom, boom!

The ants go marching four by four.
Hurrah! Hurrah!
The ants go marching four by four.
Hurrah! Hurrah!
The ants go marching four by four,
The little one stops to ask for more,
And they all go marching
Down
Into the ground
To get out
Of the rain.
Boom, boom, boom!

The ants go marching five by five.
Hurrah! Hurrah!
The ants go marching five by five.
Hurrah! Hurrah!
The ants go marching five by five,
The little one stops to jump and dive,
And they all go marching
Down
Into the ground
To get out
Of the rain.
Boom, boom, boom!

The ants go marching six by six.
Hurrah! Hurrah!

The ants go marching six by six.
Hurrah! Hurrah!
The ants go marching six by six,
The little one stops to pick up sticks,
And they all go marching
Down
Into the ground
To get out
Of the rain.
Boom, boom, boom!

The ants go marching seven by seven.
Hurrah! Hurrah!
The ants go marching seven by seven.
Hurrah! Hurrah!
The ants go marching seven by seven,
The little one stops to write with a pen,
And they all go marching
Down
Into the ground
To get out
Of the rain.
Boom, boom, boom!

The ants go marching eight by eight.
Hurrah! Hurrah!
The ants go marching eight by eight.
Hurrah! Hurrah!
The ants go marching eight by eight,
The little one stops to roller skate,
And they all go marching
Down
Into the ground
To get out
Of the rain.
Boom, boom, boom!

The ants go marching nine by nine.
Hurrah! Hurrah!

The ants go marching nine by nine.
Hurrah! Hurrah!
The ants go marching nine by nine,
The little one stops to drink and dine,
And they all go marching
Down
Into the ground
To get out
Of the rain.
Boom, boom, boom!

The ants go marching ten by ten.
Hurrah! Hurrah!
The ants go marching ten by ten.
Hurrah! Hurrah!
The ants go marching ten by ten,
The little one stops to shout
"THE END!!"

The Cock Crows in the Morning

The cock crows in the morning,
To tell us to rise,
And he that lies late
Will never be wise;
For early to bed,
And early to rise,
Is the way to be healthy
And wealthy and wise.

Alternative

The Cock Doth Crow

The cock doth crow,
To let you know,
If you be wise,
'Tis time to rise.

The Farmer in the Dell

The farmer in the dell,
The farmer in the dell,
Hi-ho, the derry-o,
The farmer in the dell.

The farmer takes a wife,
The farmer takes a wife,
Hi-ho, the derry-o,
The farmer takes a wife.

The wife takes a child,
The wife takes a child,
Hi-ho, the derry-o,
The wife takes a child.

The child takes a nurse,
The child takes a nurse,
Hi-ho, the derry-o,
The child takes a nurse.

The nurse takes the cow,
The nurse takes the cow,
Hi-ho, the derry-o,
The nurse takes the cow.

The cow takes a dog,
The cow takes a dog,
Hi-ho, the derry-o,
The cow takes a dog.

The dog takes a cat,
The dog takes a cat,
Hi-ho, the derry-o,
The dog takes a cat.

The cat takes a rat,
The cat takes a rat,
Hi-ho, the derry-o,
The cat takes a rat.

The rat takes the cheese,
The rat takes the cheese,
Hi-ho, the derry-o,
The rat takes the cheese.

The cheese stands alone,
The cheese stands alone,
Hi-ho, the derry-o,
The cheese stands alone.

The Littlest Worm

The littlest worm
(The littlest worm)
You ever saw
(You ever saw)
Got stuck inside
(Got stuck inside)
My soda straw
(My soda staw)
The littlest worm you ever saw
Got stuck inside my straw

He said to me
(He said to me)
"Don't take a sip
("Don't take a sip)
'Cause if you do
('Cause if you do)
You'll get real sick"
(You'll get real sick")
He said to me, "Don't take a sip,
'Cause if you do, you'll get real sick."

So lip to lip
(So lip to lip)
And squirm to squirm
(And squirm to squirm)
Try drinking so-
(Try drinking so-)
da through a worm.

(da through a worm.)
So lip to lip and squirm to squirm,
Try drinking soda through a worm.

I took a sip
(I took a sip)
And he went down
(And he went down)
Right through my pipe
(Right through my pipe)
He must have drowned
(He must have drowned)
I took a sip and he went down,
Right through my pipe, he must have drowned.

He was my pal
(He was my pal)
He was my friend
(He was my friend)
There is no more
(There is no more)
This is the end
(This is the end)
He was my pal, he was my friend,
There is no more, this is the end.

Now don't you fret
(Now don't you fret)
Now don't you fear
(Now don't you fear)
That little worm
(That little worm)
Had scuba gear
(Had scuba gear)
Now don't fret, now don't you fear,
That little worm had scuba gear.

The Man in the Moon

The man in the moon,
Looked out of the moon.
And this is what he said,
"Tis time that, now I'm getting up,
All babies went to bed."

Alternative

The man in the moon came tumbling down
And asked his way to Norwich;
He went by the south and burnt his mouth,
With supping cold pease porridge.

The Mulberry Bush

Here we go 'round the mulberry bush,
The mulberry bush,
The mulberry bush.
Here we go 'round the mulberry bush,
So early in the morning.

These are the chores we'll do this week,
Do this week,
Do this week.
These are the chores we'll do this week,
So early every morning.

This is the way we wash our clothes,
Wash our clothes,
Wash our clothes.
This is the way we wash our clothes,
So early Monday morning.

This is the way we iron our clothes,
Iron our clothes,

Iron our clothes.
This is the way we iron our clothes,
So early Tuesday morning.

This is the way we scrub the floor,
Scrub the floor,
Scrub the floor.
This is the way we scrub the floor,
So early Wednesday morning.

This is the way we mend our clothes,
Mend our clothes,
Mend our clothes.
This is the way we mend our clothes,
So early Thursday morning.

This is the way we sweep the floor,
Sweep the floor,
Sweep the floor.
This is the way we sweep the floor,
So early Friday morning.

This is the way we bake our bread,
Bake our bread,
Bake our bread.
This is the way we bake our bread,
So early Saturday morning.

This is the way we get dressed up,
Get dressed up,
Get dressed up.
This is the way we get dressed up,
So early Sunday morning.

Here we go 'round the mulberry bush,
The mulberry bush,
The mulberry bush.
Here we go 'round the mulberry bush,
So early in the morning.

Alternative

Here we go round the mulberry bush,
The mulberry bush, the mulberry bush,
Here we go round the mulberry bush.
On a cold and frosty morning.

This is the way we wash our hands,
Wash our hands, wash our hands,
This is the way we wash our hands,
On a cold and frosty morning.

This is the way we wash our clothes,
Wash our hands, wash our clothes,
This is the way we wash our clothes,
On a cold and frosty morning.

This is the way we go to school,
Go to school, go to school,
This is the way we go to school,
On a cold and frosty morning.

This is the way we come out of school,
Come out of school, Come out of school,
This is the way we come out of school,
On a cold and frosty morning.

The Wheels on the Bus

The wheels on the bus go round and round,
Round and round,
Round and round.
The wheels on the bus go round and round,
All through the town.

The wipers on the bus go swish, swish, swish,
Swish, swish, swish,
Swish, swish, swish.
The wipers on the bus go swish, swish, swish,
All through the town.

The doors on the bus go open and shut,
Open and shut,
Open and shut.
The doors on the bus go open and shut,
All through the town.

The horn on the bus goes beep, beep, beep,
Beep, beep, beep,
Beep, beep, beep.
The horn on the bus goes beep, beep, beep,
All through the town.

The gas on the bus goes glug, glug, glug,
Glug, glug, glug,
Glug, glug, glug.

The gas on the bus goes glug, glug, glug,
All through the town.

The money on the bus goes clink, clink, clink,
Clink, clink, clink,
Clink, clink, clink.
The money on the bus goes clink, clink, clink,
All through the town.

The driver on the bus says "Move on back,
Move on back,
Move on back."
The driver on the bus says "Move on back"
All through the town.

The baby on the bus says "Wah, wah, wah,
Wah, wah, wah,
Wah, wah, wah."
The baby on the bus says "Wah, wah, wah",
All through the town.

The people on the bus says "Shh, shh, shh,
Shh, shh, shh,
Shh, shh, shh."
The people on the bus say "Shh, shh, shh"
All through the town.

The mommy on the bus says "I love you,
I love you,
I love you."
The daddy on the bus says "I love you, too"
All through the town.

Note:

This can be an action song by using hand motions to
go along with each verse.

Variations

You can also add in more versus, with the following:

The bell on the bus goes ding, ding, ding,
Ding, ding, ding,
Ding, ding, ding.
The bell on the bus goes ding, ding, ding,
All through the town.

The lady on the bus says "Get off my feet,
Get off my feet,
Get off my feet."
The lady on the bus says "Get off my feet"
All through the town.

The people on the bus say "We had a nice ride,
We had a nice ride,
We had a nice ride."
The people on the bus say "We had a nice ride"
All through the town.

"Your name" on the bus says "Let me off,
Let me off,
Let me off!"
"Your name" on the bus says "Let me off"
All through the town.

There Was A Crooked Man

There was a crooked man,
Who walked a crooked mile.
He found a crooked sixpence,
Against a crooked stile.
He bought a crooked cat,
Which caught a crooked mouse.
And they all lived together,
In a crooked little house.

There Was A Little Turtle

There was a little turtle,
Who lived in a box.
He swam in the puddles,
And climbed on the rocks.

He snapped at the mosquito,
He snapped at the flea.
He snapped at the minnow,
And he snapped at me.

He caught the mosquito,
He caught the flea.
He caught the minnow,
But he didn't catch me!

There Was An Old Woman
Who Lived In A Shoe

There was an old woman
Who lived in a shoe.
She had so many children,
She didn't know what to do.
She gave them some broth,
Without any bread,
Whipped them all soundly,
And sent them to bed.

There's a Hole in the Middle of the Sea

There's a hole in the middle of the sea.
There's a hole in the middle of the sea.
There's a hole, there's a hole,
There's a hole in the middle of the sea.

There's a log in the hole in the middle of the sea.
There's a log in the hole in the middle of the sea.
There's a log, there's a log,
There's a log in the hole in the middle of the sea.

There's a bump on the log in the hole,
In the middle of the sea.
There's a bump on the log in the hole,
In the middle of the sea.
There's a bump, there's a bump,
There's a bump on the log in the hole,
In the middle of the sea.

There's a frog on the bump on the log,
In the hole in the middle of the sea.
There's a frog on the bump on the log,
In the hole in the middle of the sea.
There's a frog, there's a frog,
There's a frog on the bump on the log,
In the hole in the middle of the sea.

There's a fly on the frog on the bump on the log,
In the hole in the middle of the sea.
There's a fly on the frog on the bump on the log,
In the hole in the middle of the sea.
There's a fly, there's a fly,
There's a fly on the frog on the bump on the log,
In the hole in the middle of the sea.

There's a wing on the fly on the frog,
On the bump on the log in the hole,
In the middle of the sea.
There's a wing on the fly on the frog,

On the bump on the log in the hole,
In the middle of the sea.
There's a wing, there's a wing,
There's a wing on the fly on the frog,
On the bump on the log in the hole,
In the middle of the sea.

There's a flea on the wing on the fly,
On the frog on the bump on the log,
In the hole in the middle of the sea.
There's a flea on the wing on the fly,
On the frog on the bump on the log,
In the hole in the middle of the sea.
There's a flea, there's a flea,
There's a flea on the wing on the fly,
On the frog on the bump on the log,
In the hole in the middle of the sea.

This is the House That Jack Built

This is the house that Jack built.
This is the malt that lay in the house that Jack built.
This is the rat that ate the malt,
That lay in the house that Jack built.

This is the cat that killed the rat,
That ate the malt that lay in the house that Jack built.
This is the dog that worried that cat,
That killed the rat that ate the malt,
That lay in the house that Jack built.

This is the cow with the crumpled horn,
That tossed the dog that worried the cat,
That killed the rat that ate the malt,
That lay in the house that Jack built.

This is the maiden all forlorn,
That milked the cow with the crumpled horn,
That tossed the dog that worried the cat,
That killed the rat that ate the malt,
That lay in the house that Jack built.

This is the man all tattered and torn,
That kissed the maiden all forlorn,
That milked the cow with the crumpled horn,

That tossed the dog that worried the cat,
That killed the rat that ate the malt,
That lay in the house that Jack built.

This is the priest all shaven and shorn,
That married the man all tattered and torn,
That kissed the maiden all forlorn,
That milked the cow with the crumpled horn,
That tossed the dog that worried the cat,
That killed the rat that ate the malt,
That lay in the house that Jack built.

This is the cock that crowed in the morn,
That waked the priest all shaven and shorn,
That married the man all tattered and torn,
That kissed the maiden all forlorn,
That milked the cow with the crumpled horn,
That tossed the dog that worried the cat,
That killed the rat that ate the malt,
That lay in the house that Jack built.

This is the farmer sowing his corn,
That kept the cock that crowed in the morn,
That waked the priest all shaven and shorn,
That married the man all tattered and torn,
That kissed the maiden all forlorn,
That milked the cow with the crumpled horn,
That tossed the dog that worried the cat,
That killed the rat that ate the malt,
That lay in the house that Jack built!

This Little Froggy

This little froggy took a big leap,
This little froggy took a small leap,
This little froggy leaped sideways,
And this little froggy didn't leap any way,
And this little froggy went,
Hippity, hippity, hippity hop,
All the way home.

This Little Piggy

This little piggy went to the market,
This little piggy stayed home,
This little piggy had roast beef,
This little piggy had none,
And this little piggy cried,
"Wee, wee, wee,"
All the way home.

This Old Man

This old man, he
played one,
He played knick
knack with his
thumb,
With a knick,
knack, paddy whack,
Give the dog a bone;
This old man came
rolling home.

This old man, he played two,
He played knick knack with my
shoe,
With a knick, knack, paddy whack,
Give the dog a bone;
This old man came rolling home.

This old man, he played three,
He played knick knack on my knee,
With a knick, knack, paddy whack,
Give the dog a bone;
This old man came rolling home.

This old man, he played four,
He played knick knack at my door,
With a knick, knack, paddy whack,
Give the dog a bone;
This old man came rolling home.

This old man, he played five,
He played knick knack, jazz and jive,
With a knick, knack, paddy whack,
Give the dog a bone;
This old man came rolling home.

This old man, he played six,
He played knick knack with his sticks,

With a knick, knack, paddy whack,
Give the dog a bone;
This old man came rolling home.

This old man, he played seven,
He played knick knack with his pen,
With a knick, knack, paddy whack,
Give the dog a bone;
This old man came rolling home.

This old man, he played eight,
He played knick knack on my gate,
With a knick, knack, paddy whack,
Give the dog a bone;
This old man came rolling home.

This old man, he played nine,
He played knick knack, rise and shine,
With a knick, knack, paddy whack,
Give the dog a bone;
This old man came rolling home.

This old man, he played ten,
He played knick knack in my den,
With a knick, knack, paddy whack,
Give the dog a bone;
This old man came rolling home.

This old man, he played eleven,
He played knick knack up in heaven,
With a knick, knack, paddy whack,
Give the dog a bone;
This old man came rolling home.

This old man, he played twelve,
He played knick knack, dig and delve,
With a knick, knack, paddy whack,
Give the dog a bone;
This old man came rolling home.

Three Blind Mice

Three blind mice,
Three blind mice.
See how they run,
See how they run.

They all ran after
The farmer's wife,
Who cut off their tails
With a carving knife.
Did you ever see
Such a sight in your life,
As three blind mice?

Three Little Kittens

Three little kittens,
They lost their mittens,
And they began to cry,
Oh, mother, dear,
We sadly fear,
Our mittens we have lost.

What! Lost your mittens,
You naughty kittens,
Then you shall have no pie.
Meow, meow,
Then you shall have no pie.

The three little kittens,
They found their mittens,
And they began to cry,
Oh, mother, dear,
See here, see here,
Our mittens we have found.

What, found your mittens,
Then you're good kittens,
And you shall have some pie.

Purr-rr, purr-rr,
Then you shall have some pie.

Three little kittens,
Put on their mittens,
And soon ate up the pie.
Oh, mother, dear,
We sadly fear,
Our mittens we have soiled.

What! Soiled your mittens,
You naughty kittens,

And they began to sigh.
Meow, meow,
And they began to sigh.

The three little kittens,
They washed their mittens,
And hung them out to dry.
Oh, mother, dear,
Do you not hear,
Our mittens we have washed?

What! Washed your mittens?
Then you're good kittens!
But I smell a rat close by.
Meow, meow,
We smell a rat close by.

Variation (Short Version):

Three little kittens,
They lost their mittens,
And they began to cry,
Oh, mother, dear,
We sadly fear,
Our mittens we have lost.

Oh dear, don't fear
Come in and have some pie.

Twinkle, Twinkle, Little Star

Twinkle, twinkle, little star,
How I wonder what you are.
Up above the world so high,
Like a diamond in the sky.
Twinkle, twinkle, little star,
How I wonder what you are.

Two Little Eyes

Two little eyes to look around,
Two little ears to hear each sound,
One little nose to smell what's sweet,
One little mouth that likes to eat.

Two little eyes to look around,
Two little ears to hear each sound,
One little nose to smell what's sweet,
One little mouth that likes to eat.

Wee Willie Winkie

Wee Willie Winkie
Runs through the town,
Upstairs and downstairs
In his nightgown.
Rapping at the windows,
Crying through the lock,
"Are the children all in bed?
For it's now eight o'clock."

What Are Little Boys Made Of?

What are little boys made of?
Snips and snails,
And puppy dog tails,
That's what little boys are made of.

What Are Little Girls Made Of?

What are little girls made of?
Sugar and spice,
And everything nice,
That's what little girls are made of.

You Are My Sunshine

You are my sunshine, my only sunshine.
You make me happy when skies are grey.
You'll never know dear, how much I love you.
Please don't take my sunshine away.

The other night dear, as I lay sleeping,
I dreamt I held you in my arms.
When I awoke dear, I was mistaken,
So I hung my head down and cried.

You are my sunshine, my only sunshine.
You make me happy when skies are grey.
You'll never know dear, how much I love you.
Please don't take my sunshine away.

End Notes

Thank you for reading. I hope you (and your children) have enjoyed all the nursery rhymes and sing-along songs!

If you enjoyed this book, please take a moment to post a review and share with your friends. If you were unsatisfied with this book, please let me know using the contact details below.

Please send me your comments and suggestions. Any feedback is greatly appreciated.

Connect with the Author Online:

http://www.smashwords.com/profile/view/JenniferEdwards

Author.JenniferEdwards@gmail.com

~~~~

Made in the USA
Lexington, KY
06 October 2015